Robo's Favorite Places
by Wade Hudson
illustrated by Cathy Johnson

Robo's Favorite Places text copyright 1999 by Wade Hudson.

Illustrations copyright 1999 by Cathy Johnson. All rights reserved.

Inquiries should be addressed to

JUST US BOOKS, INC.

356 Glenwood Ave., East Orange, NJ 07017

Printed in Mexico. First Edition

10 9 8 7 6 5 4 3 2 1

Library of Congress Cataloging in Publication Data is available.

ISBN: 0-940975-85-8

Robo likes his new teacher. Mrs. Jones makes her students use their imagination. Robo likes that.

"Everybody has a favorite place," Mrs. Jones says to the class.

"Visiting different places is exciting and fun. My favorite place is the flea market. Now class, tell me yours."

"Hmmm. What *is* my favorite place?" Robo asks himself.

"I have so many. How can I choose just one?"

"I like the library. There
are many great books that I
love to read."

"I always find tasty candy and snacks at the corner store."

"Then there is Grandpa's house.

Pop Pop likes to play tricks on me."

"The swimming pool is a cool place, especially in the summer.

It's best to learn to swim the right way."

"Skating at the rink with my friends is exciting. Well, if I don't fall down too often."

"I like zooming down
the slide at the playground.
It's fun-n-n-n-n-n!"

"Sometimes, the neighborhood playhouse has funny and scary shows. I like them all."

"I love to feed peanuts to the elephants at the zoo.

There are other interesting animals there, too. Most of them are friendly."

"The science museum is fascinating.

There are always new animal exhibits and strange experiments on display."

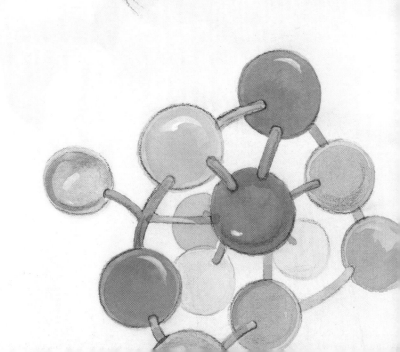

"I love the planetarium.
The sky is so beautiful.

I can look up and see
thousands of stars."

Suddenly, Robo's face brightens.

"I know my very favorite place," he says to himself.

Robo sits straight in his desk and raises his hand so Mrs. Jones can see it.

"Yes, Robo?" Mrs. Jones asks.

"I know my favorite place," Robo tells Mrs. Jones and the class.

"That's very good," Mrs. Jones says with a smile.

Robo smiles, too, because later in the afternoon he will visit his favorite place.

It's the world wide web on his home computer.

On the internet Robo can visit just about any place he likes.

ROBO'S FAVORITE PLACES
by Wade Hudson
illustrated by Cathy Johnson

Wade Hudson is the author of a number of books for chldren. Among his works are *AFRO-BETS Book of Black Heroes from A to Z* (co-authored with Valerie Wilson Wesley); *Jamal's Busy Day*; *Anthony's Big Surprise*; *AFRO-BETS Kids: I'm Gonna Be* and *In Praise of Our Fathers and Our Mothers: A Black Family Treasury by Outstanding Authors and Artists.* He lives with his wife and children in New Jersey.

Cathy Johnson is an accomplished illustrator-graphic designer. She has illustrated several books for children, including *Many Colors of Mother Goose* and *Glo Goes Shopping*. Johnson lives in Kansas City, Missouri, where she operates the graphic design studio, LUV-IT.

For my sister, Mary
who loved life and children
WH

For my wonderful son, Clinton Love Johnson
and my nephews, Corey and Alston
With Love, CJ